CROMWELL

Barney Saltzberg

ATHENEUM 1986 NEW YORK

Library of Congress Cataloging-in-Publication Data

Saltzberg, Barney.
Cromwell.

SUMMARY: Cromwell is not like other puppies, since he wears clothes and digs with a shovel, but his new owner expects him to behave like a regular dog.
[1. Dogs—Fiction] I. Title.
PZ7.S1552Cr 1986 [E] 85-20022
ISBN 0-689-31282-2

Published simultaneously in Canada by
Collier Macmillan Canada, Inc.
Composition by Boro Typographers, New York City
Printed and bound by South China Printing Company, Hong Kong
Typography by Mary Ahern
First Edition

ife Susan, who makes me smile

Special thanks to Toni Mendez & Jean Karl

When Cromwell was a puppy,
his mother could tell that
he was very special.

He wore a shirt, wool pants and little black shoes from the day he was born. Nobody knew where the clothes came from. The only one who was concerned was his mother. But she was too busy to think much about it.

Cromwell's brothers and sisters didn't really notice anything especially different about their brother.

Although they did pay attention when he read them bedtime stories.

Most of the time the puppies just went
about their own business.

Cromwell did the same.

The time came when Cromwell and his brothers and sisters were old enough to leave home. One day a man named Arthur came to choose a puppy. Arthur lived alone, and he was looking for a very special companion.
Arthur couldn't help but notice that Cromwell was wearing clothes and the other puppies weren't. He was also standing up and waving as if to say, "Pick me, pick me," which is just what Arthur did.

Cromwell waved good-bye. He was happy
to be with Arthur but sad to be leaving his family.
"I have made a place for you to sleep," Arthur
said, trying to reassure Cromwell.

Cromwell had dreamed of having
a big bed and a quilt filled
with goose feathers.

He was disappointed when he saw his new room. Arthur had given him a corduroy mat and two shiny plastic bowls. “I don’t think I’m going to like living here,” Cromwell said to himself.

That night Cromwell crept into Arthur's bedroom and quietly climbed up on the bed. He fell asleep between Arthur's feet.

In the morning, before Arthur awoke,
Cromwell tiptoed back to his corduroy
mat and changed his clothes. It was
chilly on the floor. "I don't think I
like living here," he mused.

After a while Cromwell heard
Arthur puttering about. He could
smell fresh coffee.
Sweet sounds began to float in,
filling the room, finding their
way into the cold corners where
the old gas heater couldn't reach.

Arthur was playing the cello. Cromwell had never heard such lovely music before. It was so wonderful he decided to dance.

“Maybe living here won’t be so bad after all,” Cromwell howled.

But Arthur went to work,
and the music stopped.

“The house is too quiet,” Cromwell thought to himself.

“The cello looks lonely.”

Cromwell stared up at the magnificent cello.
He wondered how he could make it play.

He climbed up the cello to get
a better look.

Before he knew what had happened,
Cromwell slipped and fell through the strings
of the cello. He wiggled and squirmed. It was
no use. Cromwell was trapped.

When evening came, Cromwell, tired and weak from a whole day of being tangled in the cello strings, looked sadly out at the first stars. "I knew I wouldn't like living here." He began to cry.

Finally Arthur came home. He heard whimpering in the living room and ran toward the sounds, afraid something terrible had happened to his new friend. He saw poor Cromwell caught in the cello. Arthur gently pulled his little puppy out from the strings. "You must have had a terrible day, my friend," Arthur said.

Cromwell was so tired he could barely keep his head up.

Arthur fed him some warm stew. That night Cromwell went to sleep with Arthur in the big bed.

It was morning again.

Cromwell could tell

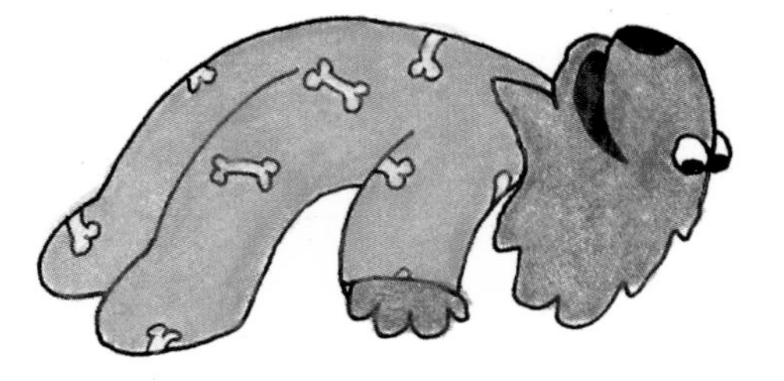

by the sweet sounds of Arthur's cello.

Arthur went off to work, and the music
stopped. But today Cromwell didn't mind. He found
a surprise in his bowl and quickly ate one
of the bones.

With the remaining two bones,
Cromwell put together
his own cello.

"Maybe living with Arthur won't be so bad after all."